STAR WARS®

INFINITIES

THE EMPIRE STRIKES BACK™

VOLUME THREE

Script
DAVE LAND

Pencils
DAVIDÉ FABBRI

Inks
CHRISTIAN DALLA VECCHIA

Colors
DAN JACKSON

Lettering
STEVE DUTRO

Cover Art
CHRIS BACHALO WITH TIM TOWNSEND AND ALEX BLEYAERT

After an encounter with bounty hunter Boba Fett in Cloud City, Han Solo, Princess Leia, and Chewbacca depart for the swamp world of Dagobah. There they hope to find Master Yoda, whom Luke mentioned with his dying breath.

A short time later, Fett's employer—Darth Vader—arrives in Cloud City. Angered that Solo and the others were not detained, Vader's Imperial forces destroy the city.

Meanwhile, on Dagobah, Yoda tells them that it is Leia, not Solo, who is to become a Jedi. He also reveals that Leia is Luke's sister—and Vader's child!

THE *STAR WARS INFINITIES* SERIES ASKS THE QUESTION: WHAT IF ONE THING HAPPENED DIFFERENTLY FROM WHAT WE SAW IN THE CLASSIC FILMS?

Spotlight

DARK HORSE COMICS

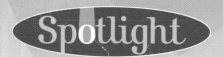

Visit us at www.abdopublishing.com

Reinforced library bound edition published in 2011 by Spotlight, a division of the ABDO Group, 8000 West 78th Street, Edina, Minnesota 55439. Spotlight produces high-quality reinforced library bound editions for schools and libraries. Published by agreement with Dark Horse Comics, Inc., and Lucasfilm Ltd.

Printed in the United States of America, North Mankato, Minnesota.
102010
012011
 This book contains at least 10% recycled materials.

Library of Congress Cataloging-in-Publication Data

Land, David.
 The empire strikes back / script, Dave Land ; art, Davidé Fabbri. -- Reinforced library bound ed.
   v. cm. -- (Star wars. Infinities)
  ISBN 978-1-59961-849-4 (vol. 1) -- ISBN 978-1-59961-850-0 (vol. 2) -- ISBN 978-1-59961-851-7 (vol. 3) -- ISBN 978-1-59961-852-4 (vol. 4)
  1. Graphic novels. [1. Graphic novels. 2. Science fiction.] I. Fabbri, Davide, ill. II. Title.
  PZ7.7.L35Emp 2011
  741.5'973--dc22
                              2010020248

All Spotlight books have reinforced library bindings and
are manufactured in the United States of America.

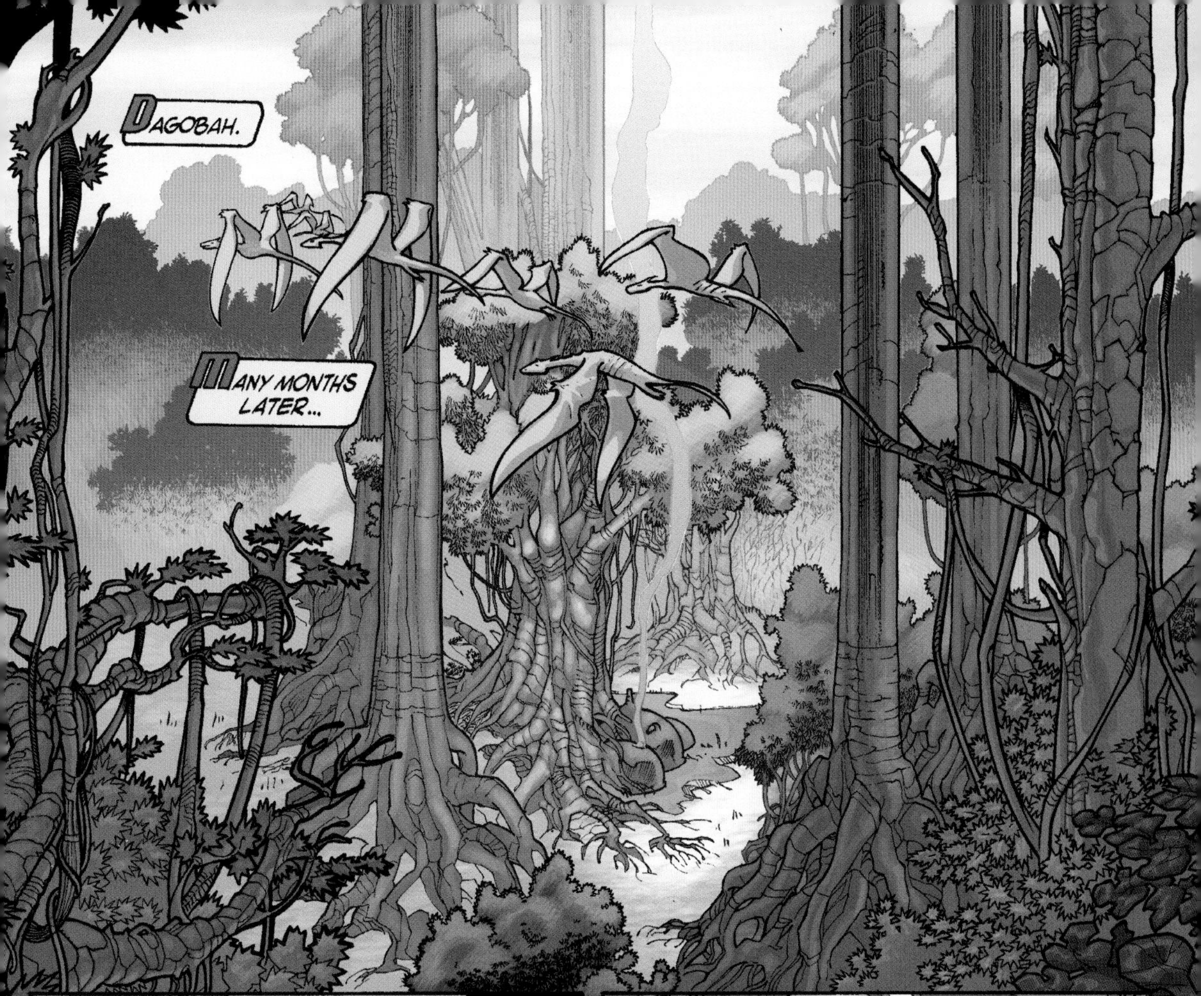
DAGOBAH.
MANY MONTHS LATER...

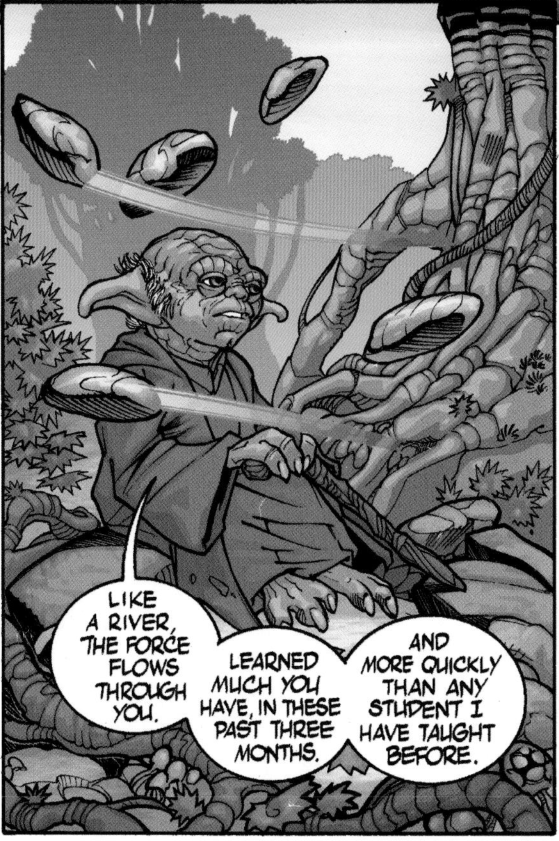
LIKE A RIVER, THE FORCE FLOWS THROUGH YOU.
LEARNED MUCH YOU HAVE, IN THESE PAST THREE MONTHS.
AND MORE QUICKLY THAN ANY STUDENT I HAVE TAUGHT BEFORE.

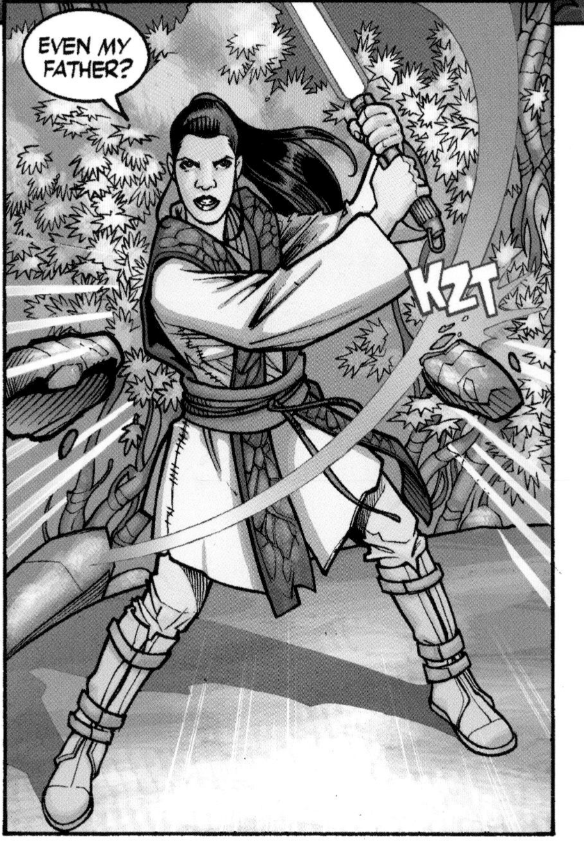
EVEN MY FATHER?
KZT

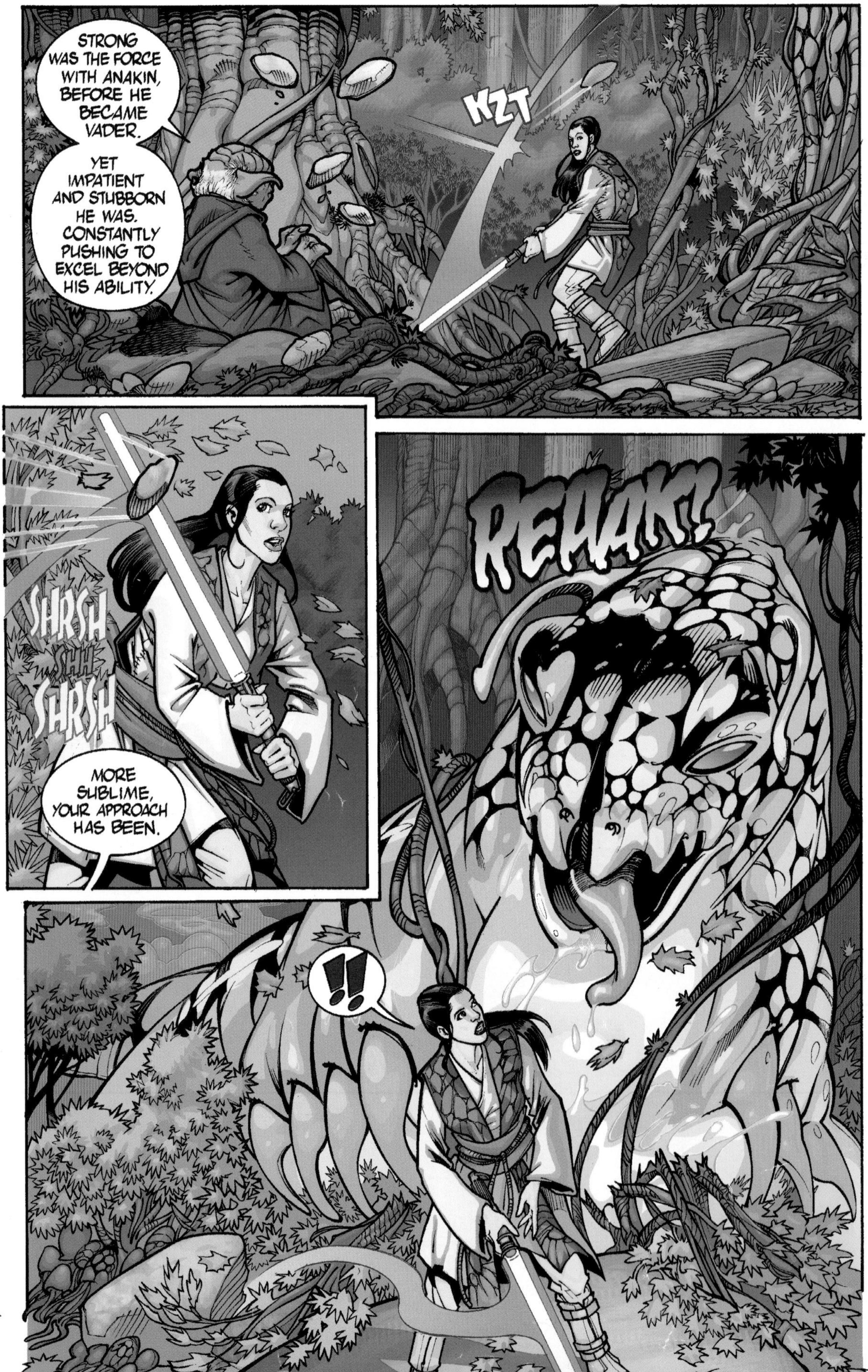
STRONG WAS THE FORCE WITH ANAKIN, BEFORE HE BECAME VADER.
YET IMPATIENT AND STUBBORN HE WAS. CONSTANTLY PUSHING TO EXCEL BEYOND HIS ABILITY.
KZT
SHRSH SHH SHRSH
MORE SUBLIME, YOUR APPROACH HAS BEEN.
REAAK!
!!

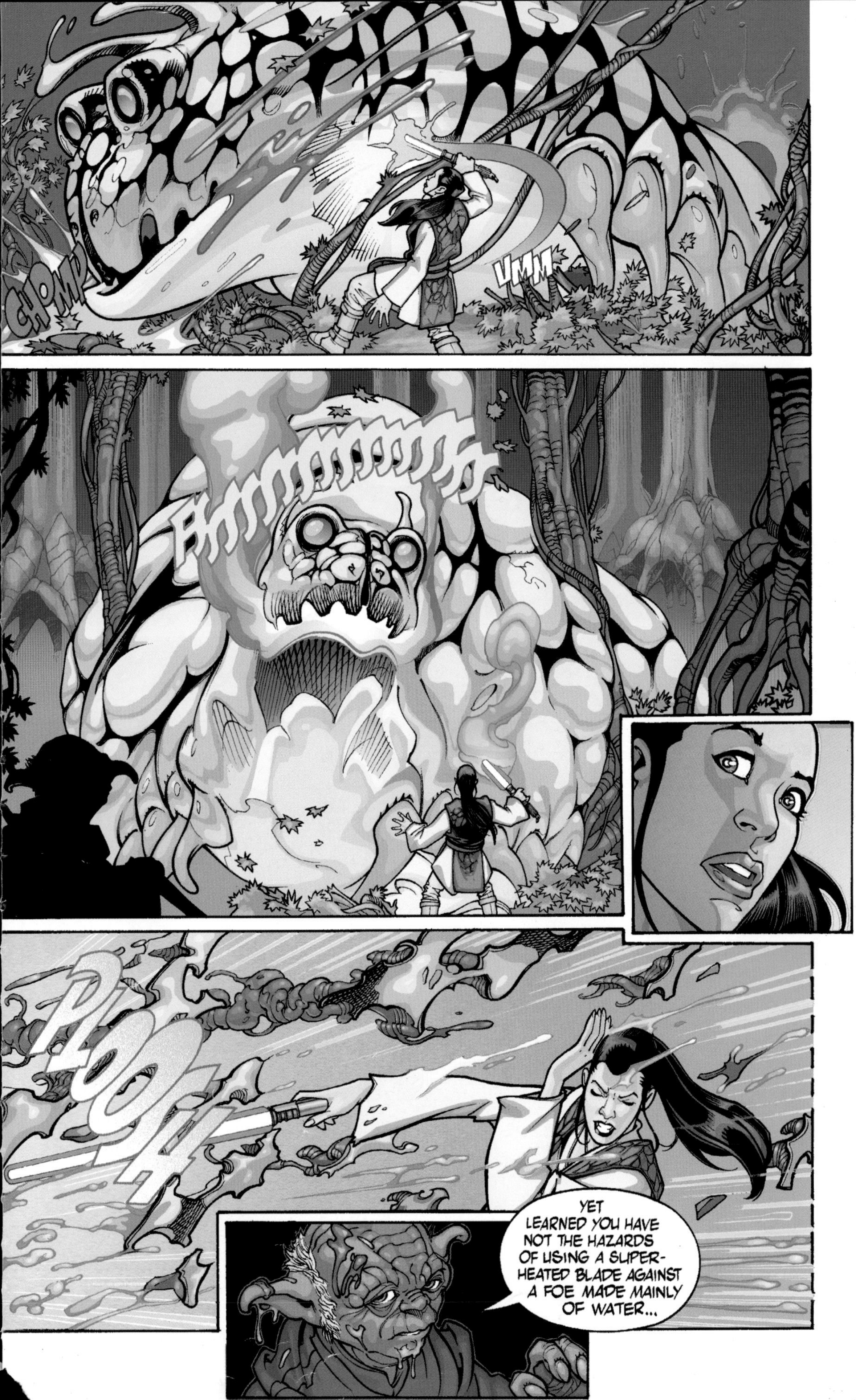
CHOMP
UMM
PLOOSH
YET LEARNED YOU HAVE NOT THE HAZARDS OF USING A SUPER-HEATED BLADE AGAINST A FOE MADE MAINLY OF WATER...

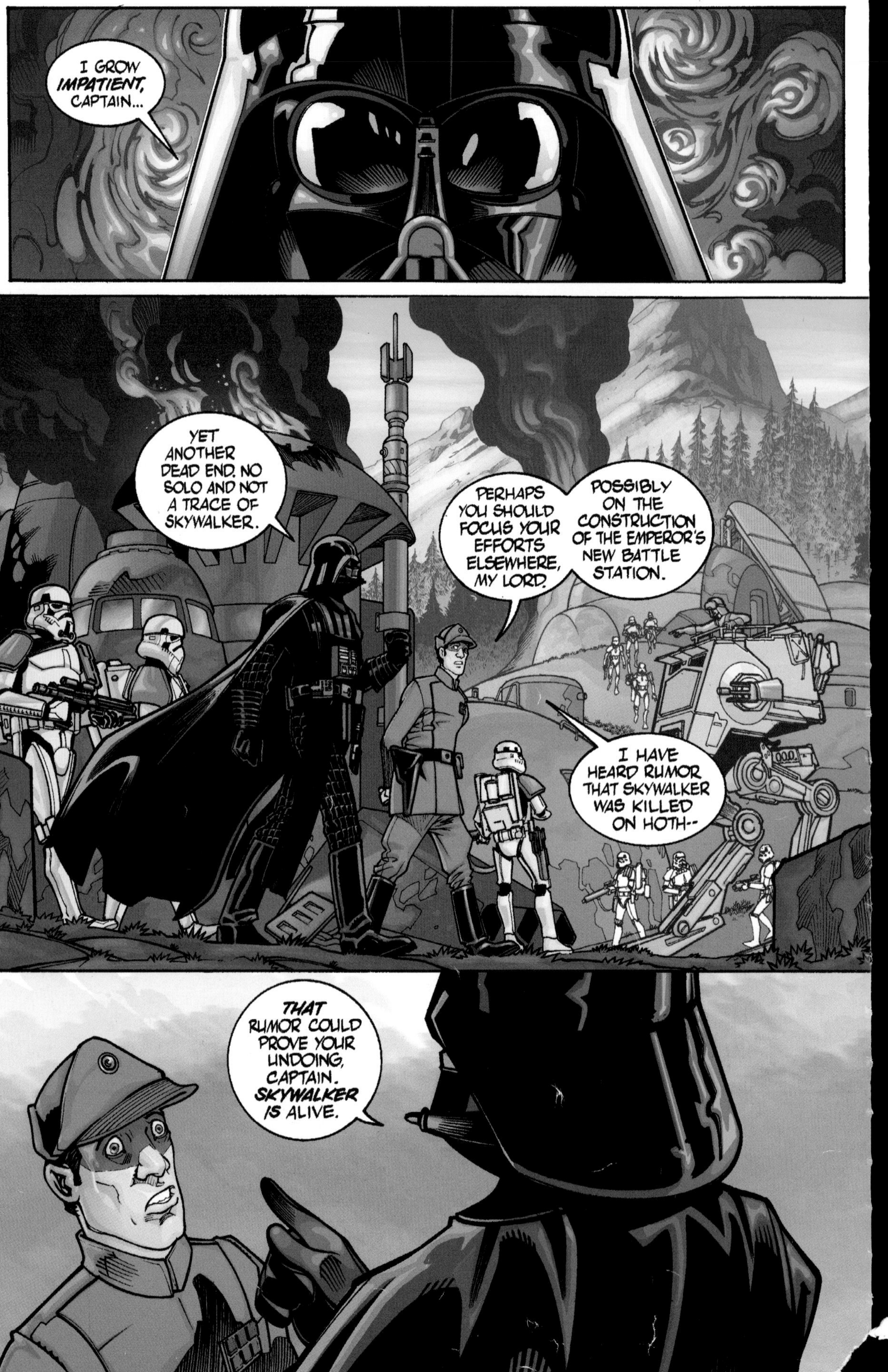
I GROW *IMPATIENT*, CAPTAIN...
YET ANOTHER DEAD END. NO SOLO AND NOT A TRACE OF SKYWALKER.
PERHAPS YOU SHOULD FOCUS YOUR EFFORTS ELSEWHERE, MY LORD.
POSSIBLY ON THE CONSTRUCTION OF THE EMPEROR'S NEW BATTLE STATION.
I HAVE HEARD RUMOR THAT SKYWALKER WAS KILLED ON HOTH--
THAT RUMOR COULD PROVE YOUR UNDOING, CAPTAIN. *SKYWALKER IS* ALIVE.

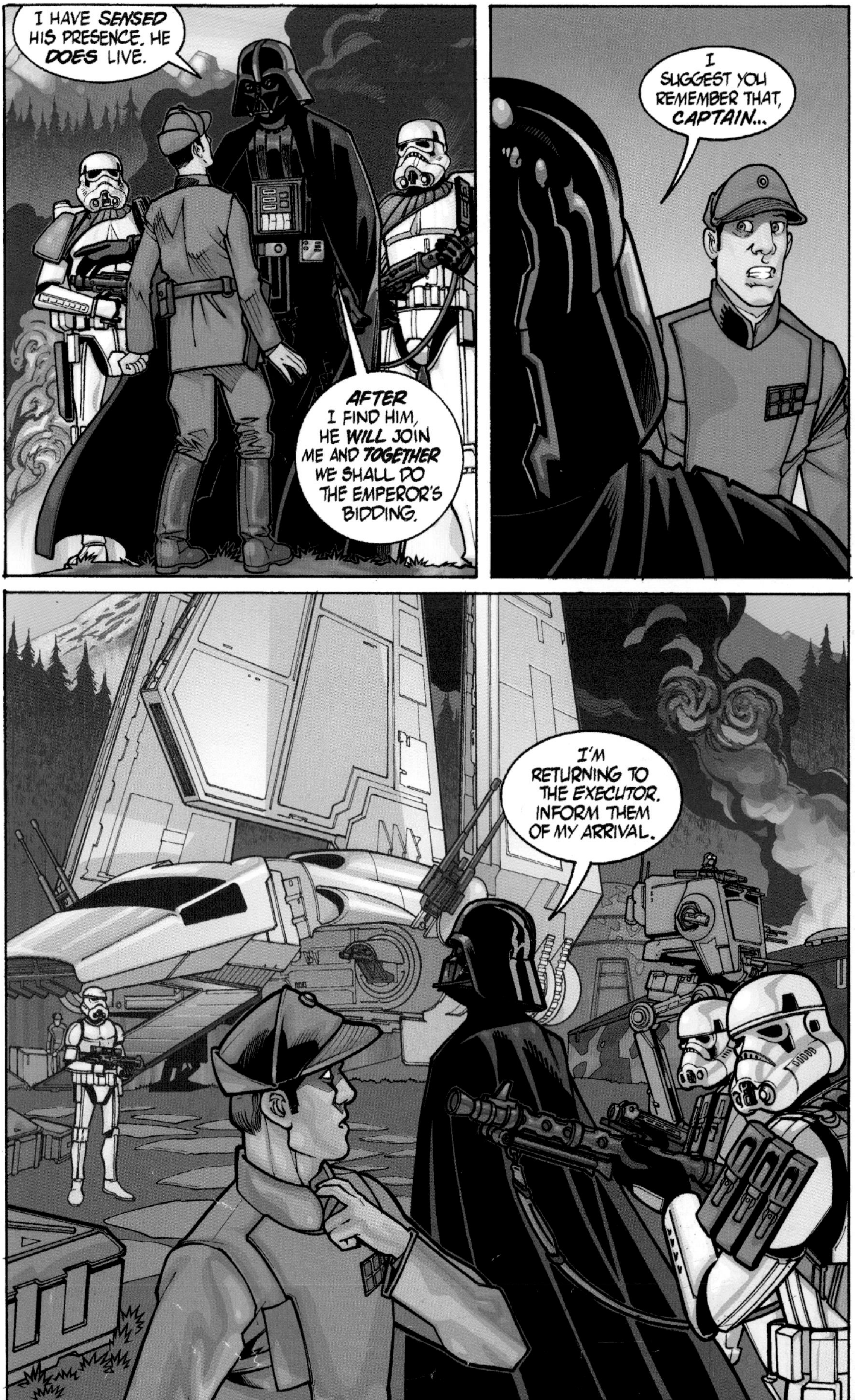
I HAVE *SENSED* HIS PRESENCE. HE *DOES* LIVE.
AFTER I FIND HIM, HE *WILL* JOIN ME AND *TOGETHER* WE SHALL DO THE EMPEROR'S BIDDING.
I SUGGEST YOU REMEMBER THAT, *CAPTAIN*...
I'M RETURNING TO THE *EXECUTOR*. INFORM THEM OF MY ARRIVAL.

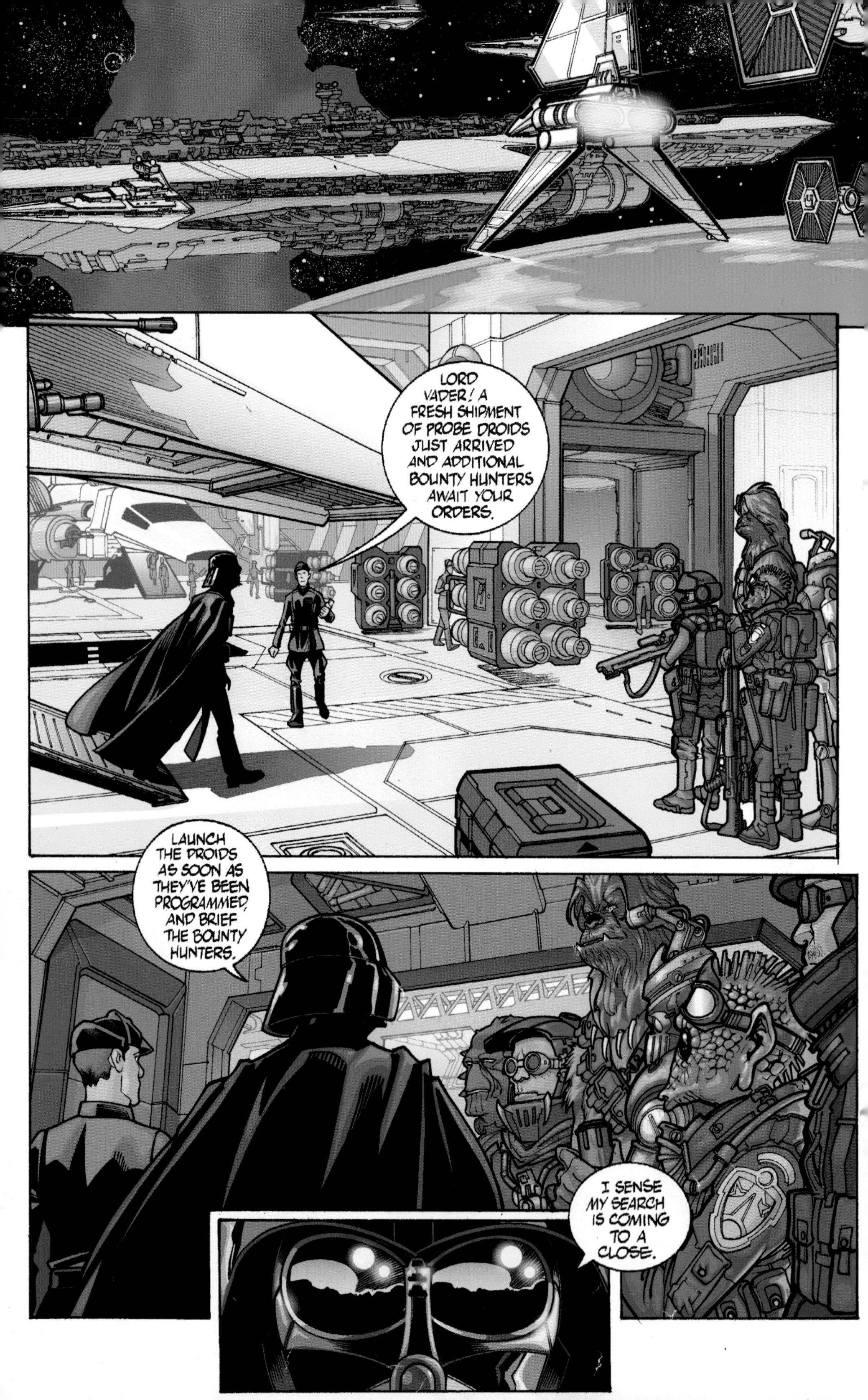
LORD VADER! A FRESH SHIPMENT OF PROBE DROIDS JUST ARRIVED AND ADDITIONAL BOUNTY HUNTERS AWAIT YOUR ORDERS.
LAUNCH THE DROIDS AS SOON AS THEY'VE BEEN PROGRAMMED, AND BRIEF THE BOUNTY HUNTERS.
I SENSE MY SEARCH IS COMING TO A CLOSE.

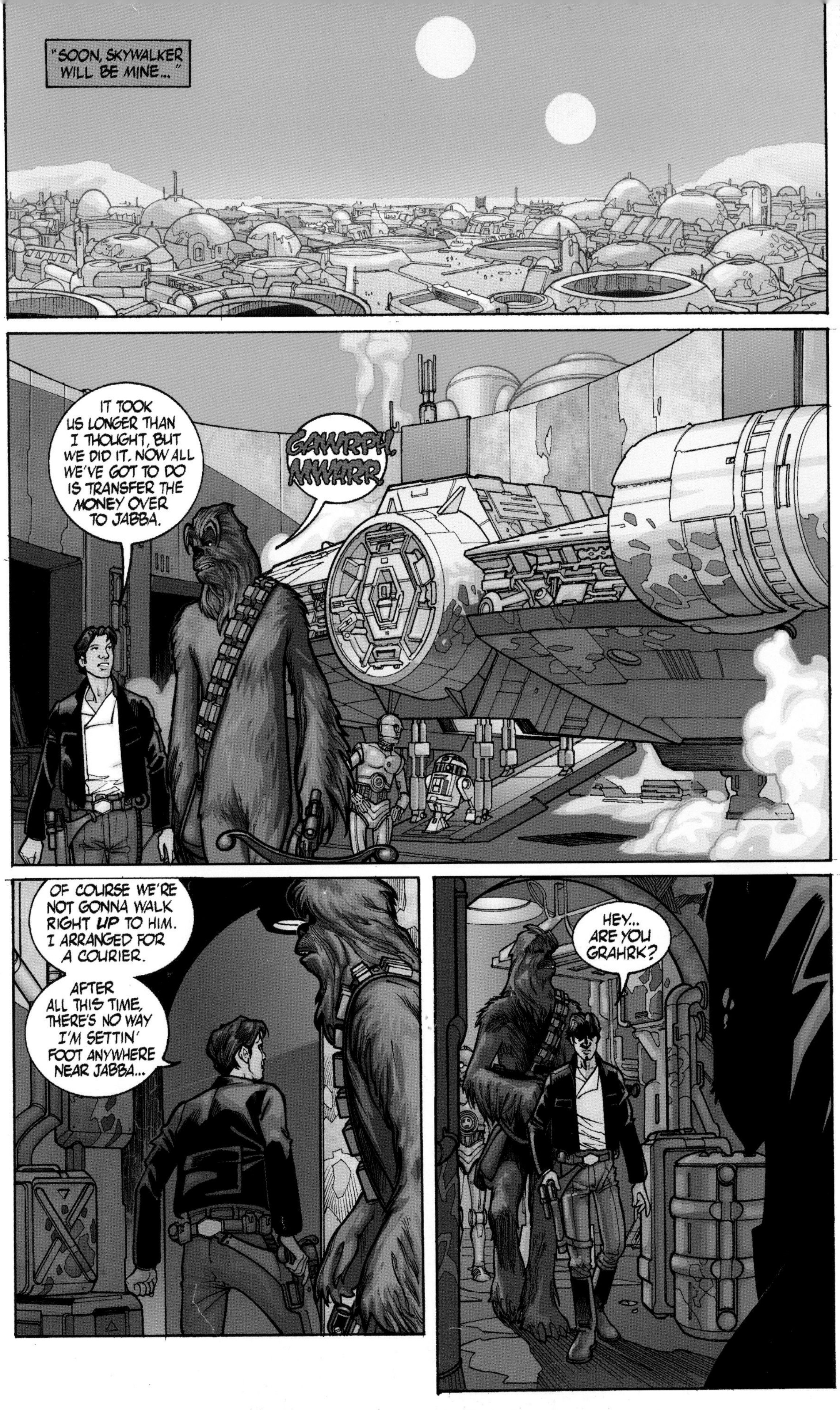
"SOON, SKYWALKER WILL BE MINE..."
IT TOOK US LONGER THAN I THOUGHT, BUT WE DID IT. NOW ALL WE'VE GOT TO DO IS TRANSFER THE MONEY OVER TO JABBA.
GAWRPH. MWARR.
OF COURSE WE'RE NOT GONNA WALK RIGHT UP TO HIM. I ARRANGED FOR A COURIER.
AFTER ALL THIS TIME, THERE'S NO WAY I'M SETTIN' FOOT ANYWHERE NEAR JABBA...
HEY... ARE YOU GRAHRK?

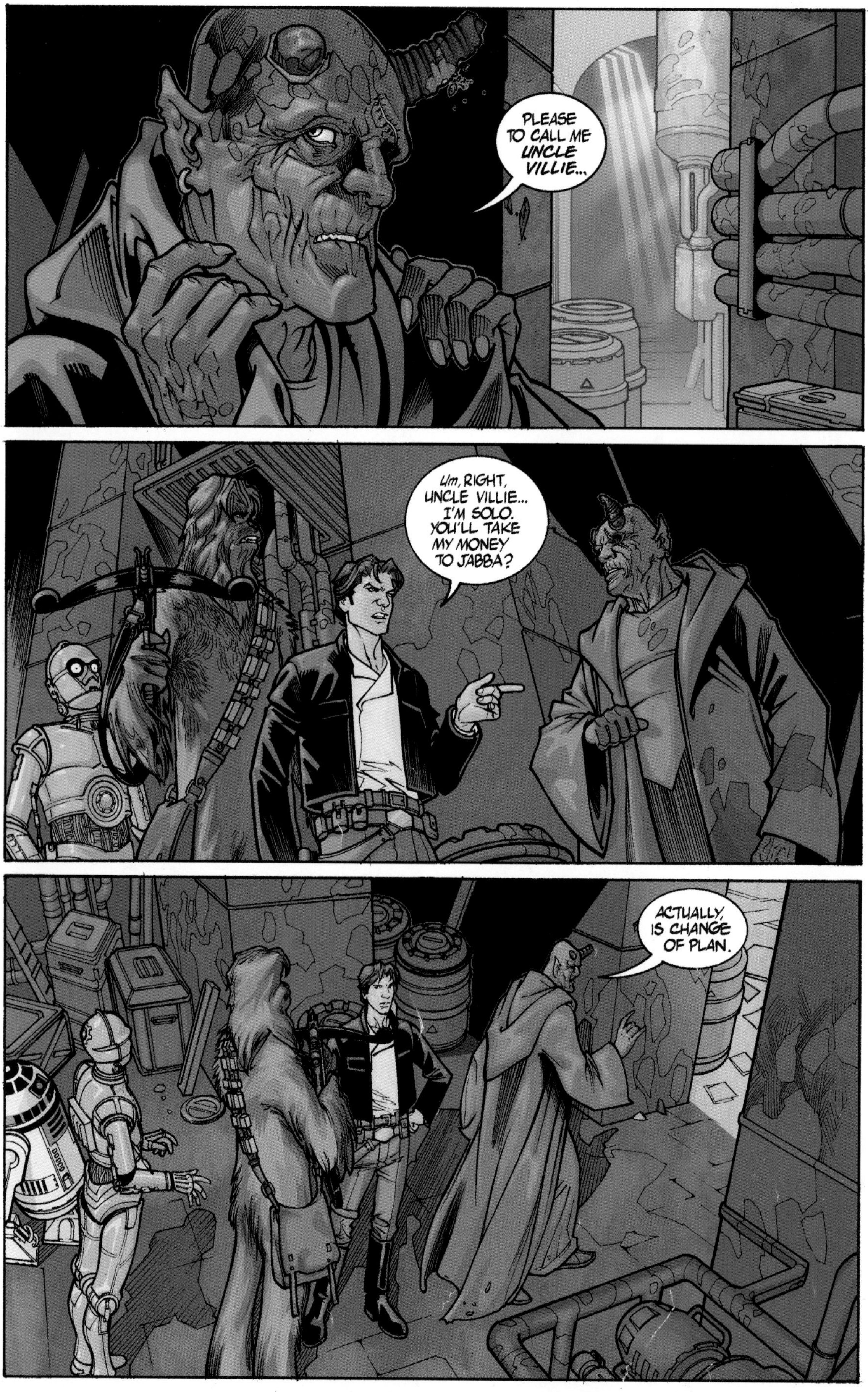
PLEASE TO CALL ME *UNCLE VILLIE*...
Um, RIGHT, UNCLE VILLIE... I'M SOLO. YOU'LL TAKE MY MONEY TO JABBA?
ACTUALLY, IS CHANGE OF PLAN.

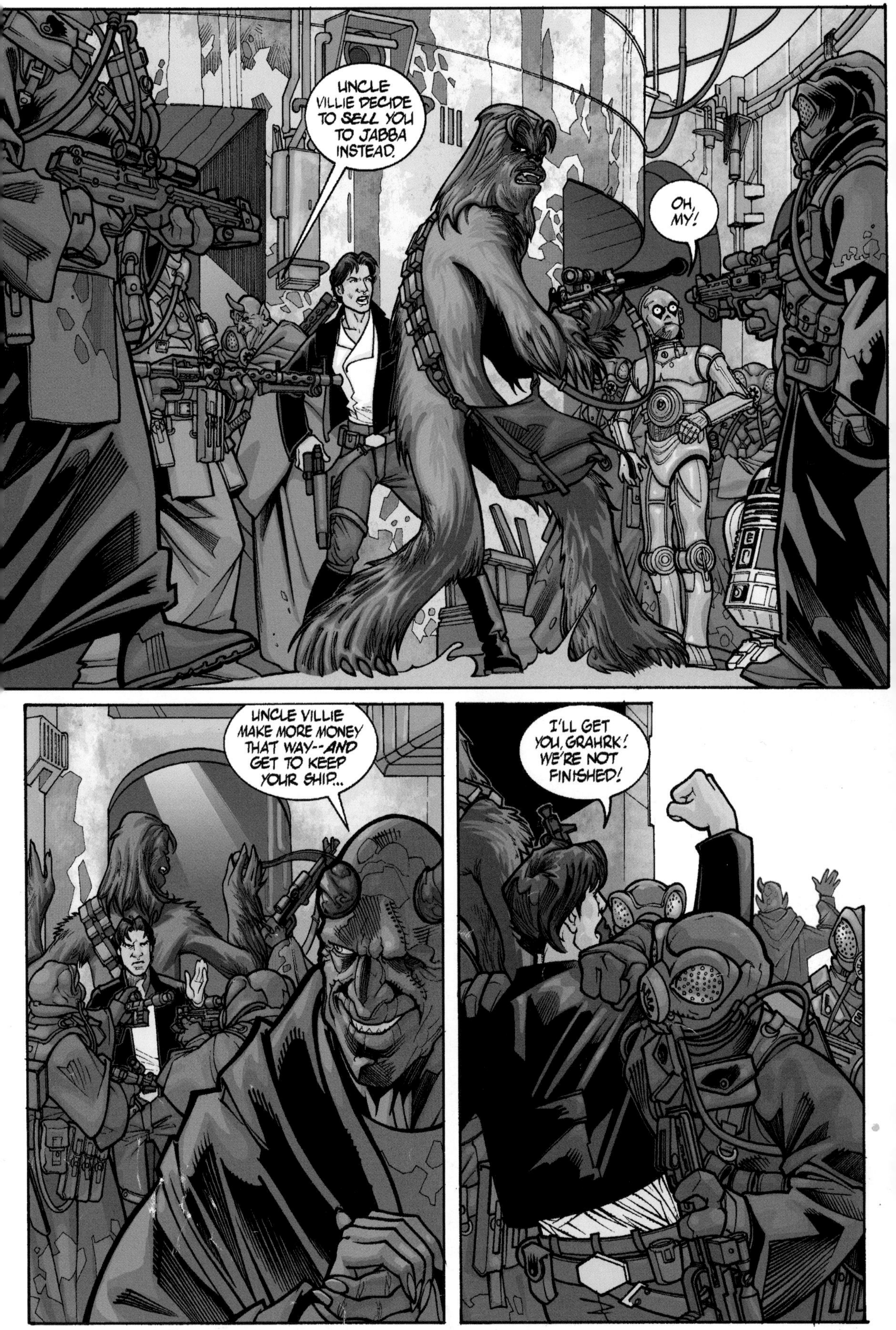
UNCLE VILLIE DECIDE TO SELL YOU TO JABBA INSTEAD.
OH, MY!
UNCLE VILLIE MAKE MORE MONEY THAT WAY--AND GET TO KEEP YOUR SHIP...
I'LL GET YOU, GRAHRK! WE'RE NOT FINISHED!

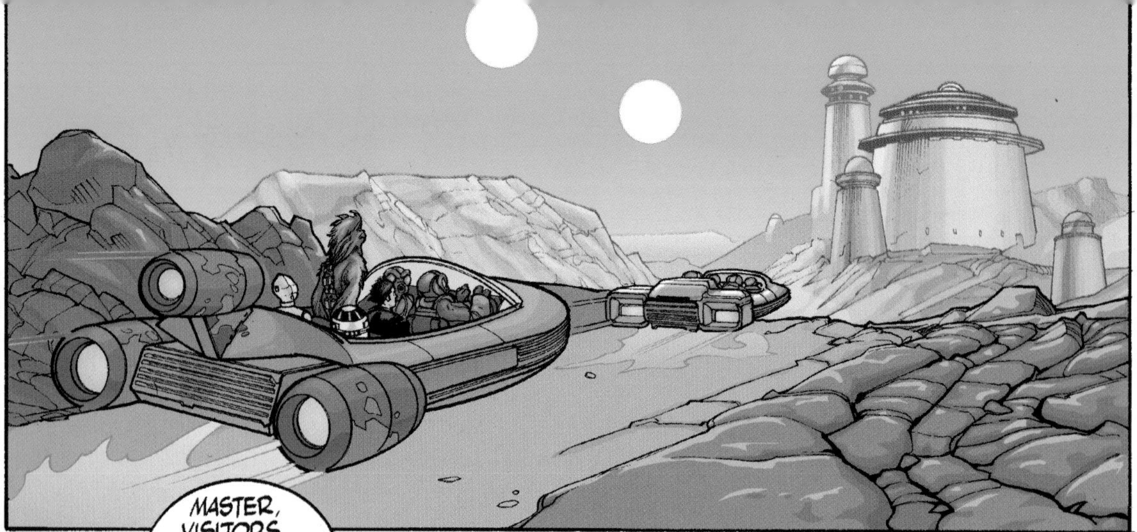

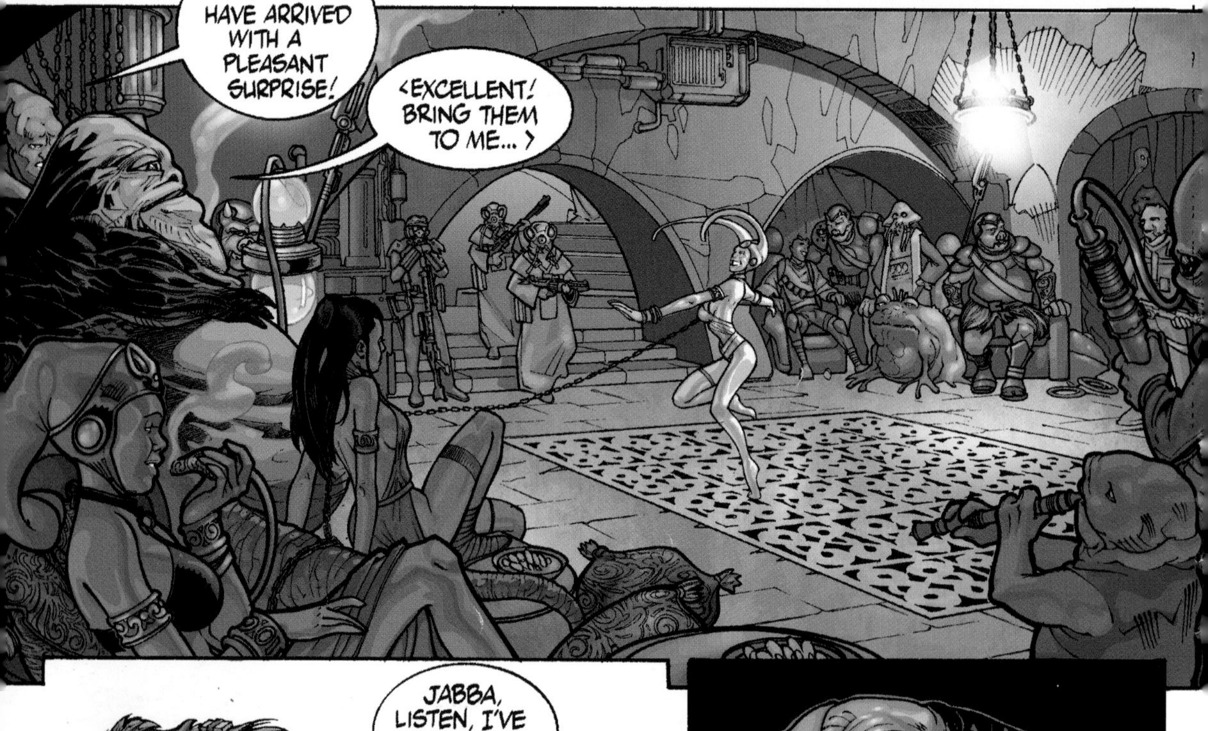
MASTER, VISITORS HAVE ARRIVED WITH A PLEASANT SURPRISE!
<EXCELLENT! BRING THEM TO ME...>

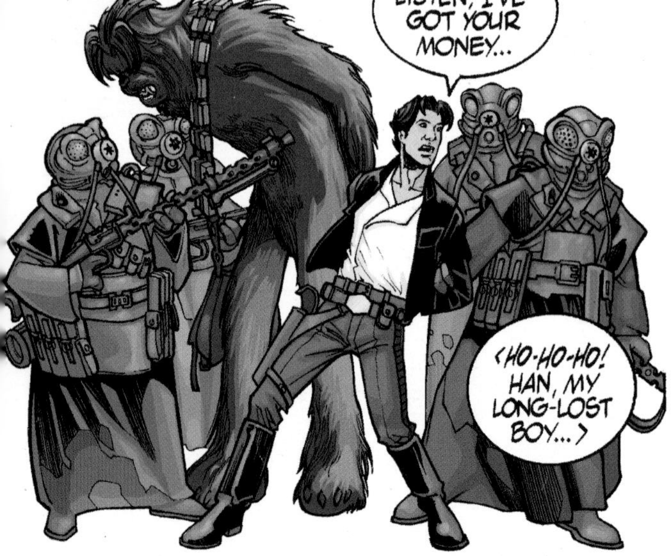
JABBA, LISTEN, I'VE GOT YOUR MONEY...
<HO-HO-HO! HAN, MY LONG-LOST BOY...>

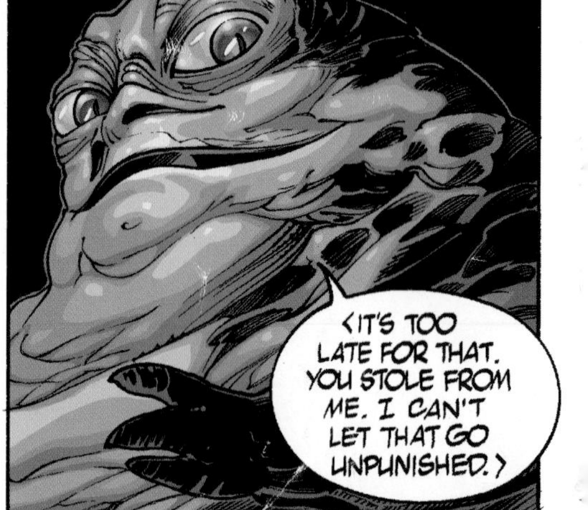
<IT'S TOO LATE FOR THAT. YOU STOLE FROM ME. I CAN'T LET THAT GO UNPUNISHED.>

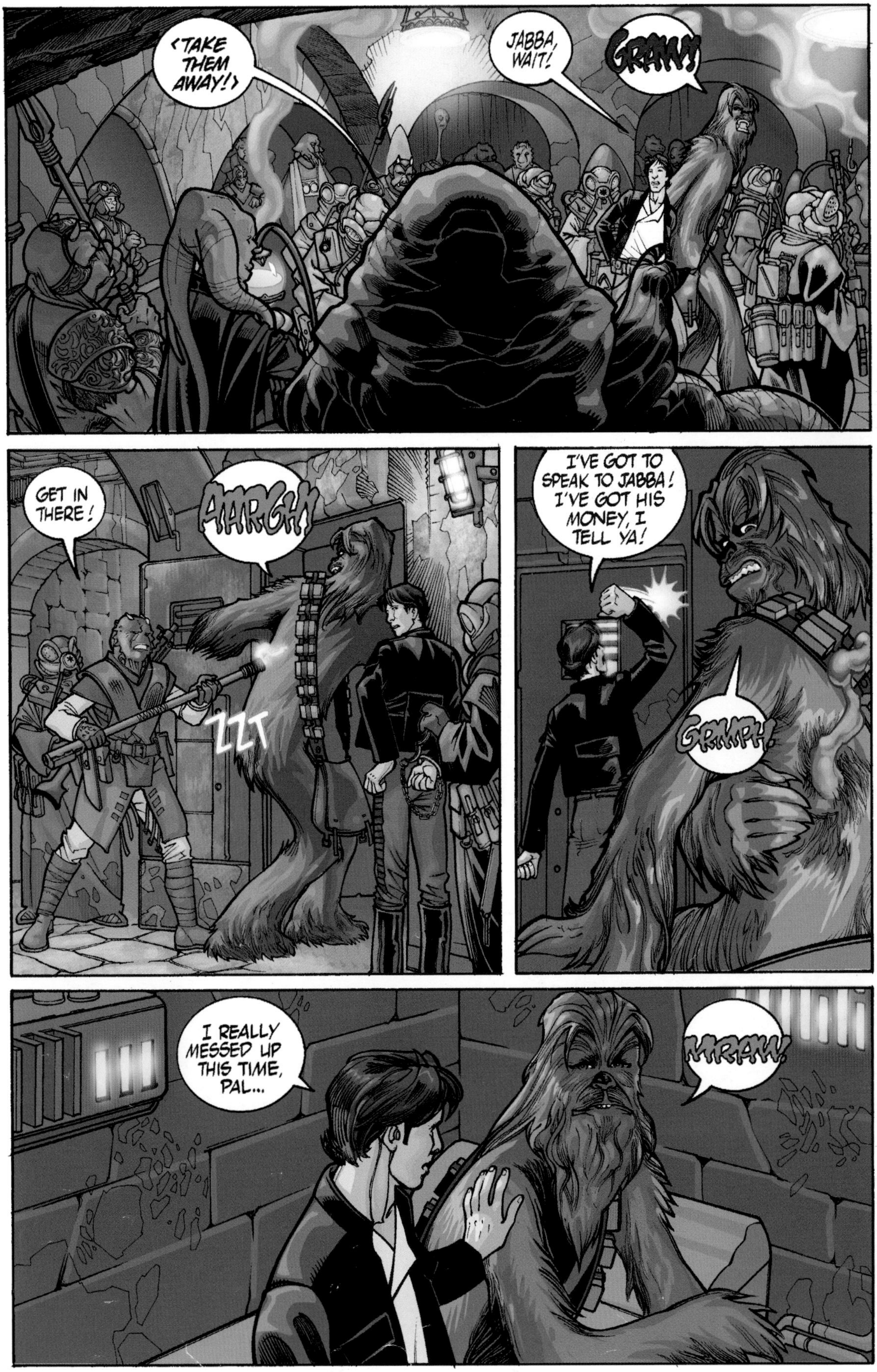
<TAKE THEM AWAY!>
JABBA, WAIT!
GRAWW!
GET IN THERE!
AARGH!
ZZT
I'VE GOT TO SPEAK TO JABBA! I'VE GOT HIS MONEY, I TELL YA!
GRMPH!
I REALLY MESSED UP THIS TIME, PAL...
MRAW!

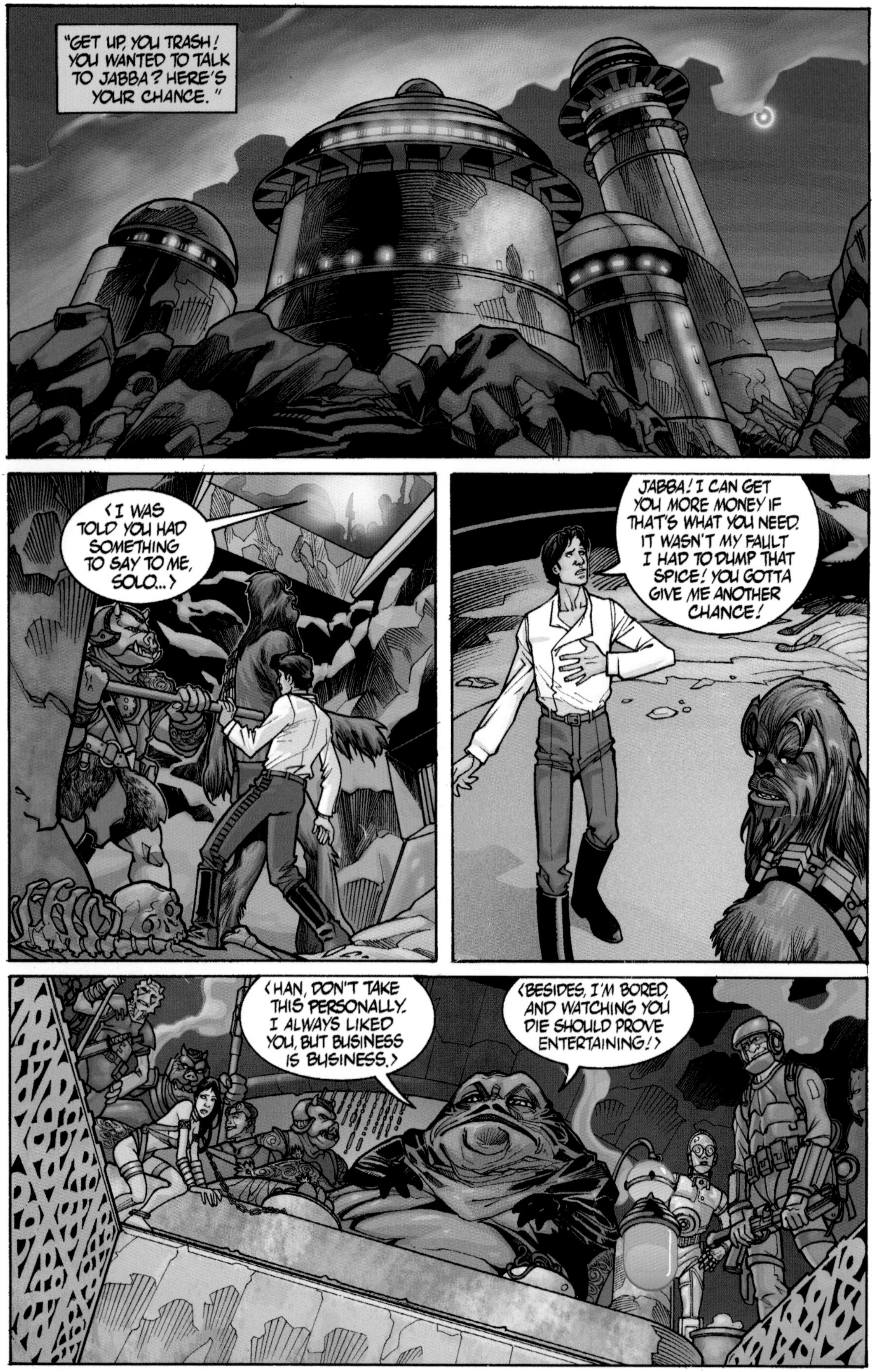
"GET UP, YOU TRASH! YOU WANTED TO TALK TO JABBA? HERE'S YOUR CHANCE."
‹I WAS TOLD YOU HAD SOMETHING TO SAY TO ME, SOLO...›
JABBA! I CAN GET YOU MORE MONEY IF THAT'S WHAT YOU NEED. IT WASN'T MY FAULT I HAD TO DUMP THAT SPICE! YOU GOTTA GIVE ME ANOTHER CHANCE!
‹HAN, DON'T TAKE THIS PERSONALLY. I ALWAYS LIKED YOU, BUT BUSINESS IS BUSINESS.›
‹BESIDES, I'M BORED, AND WATCHING YOU DIE SHOULD PROVE ENTERTAINING!›

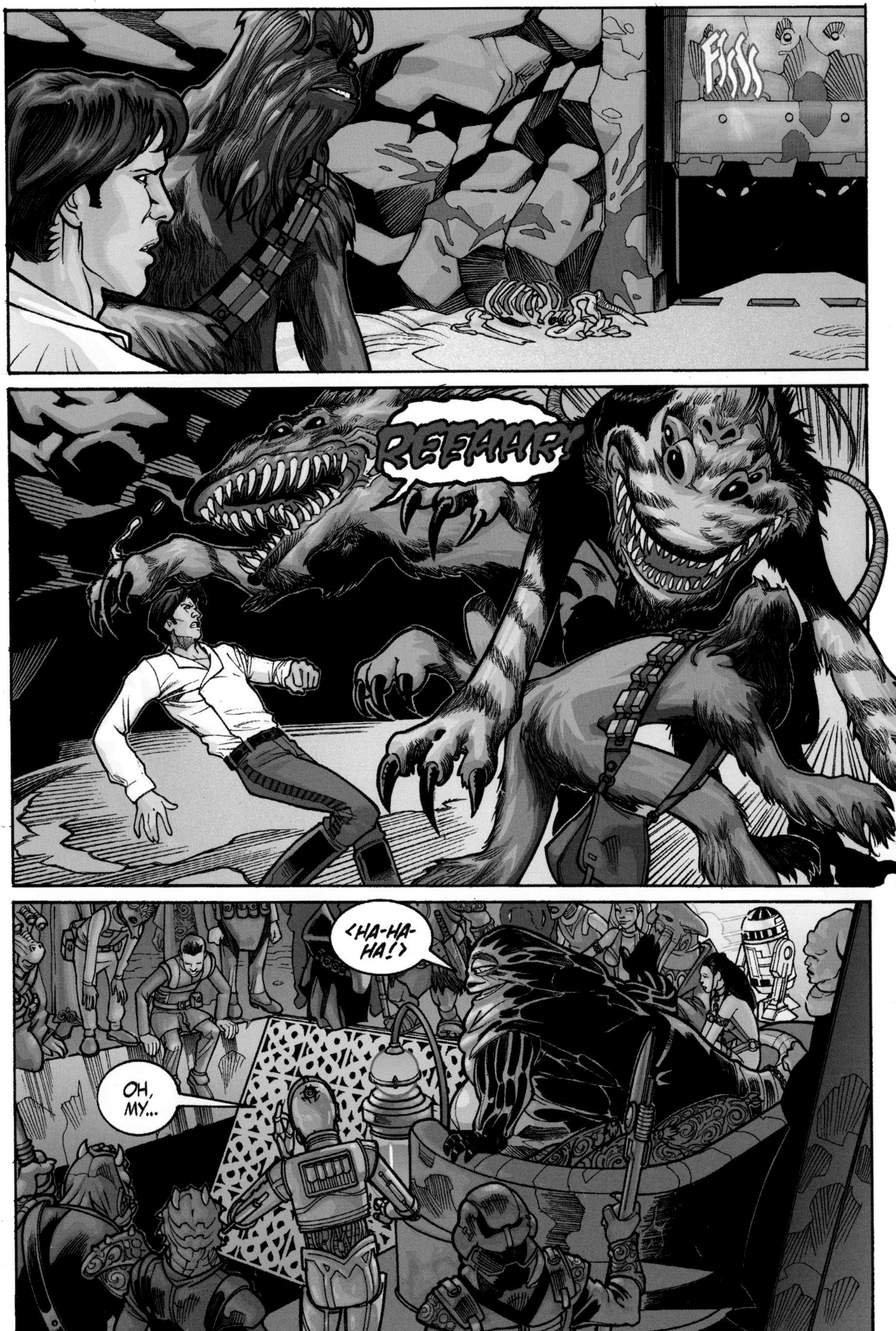
FSSS
REEAAAR!
<HA-HA-HA!>
OH, MY...

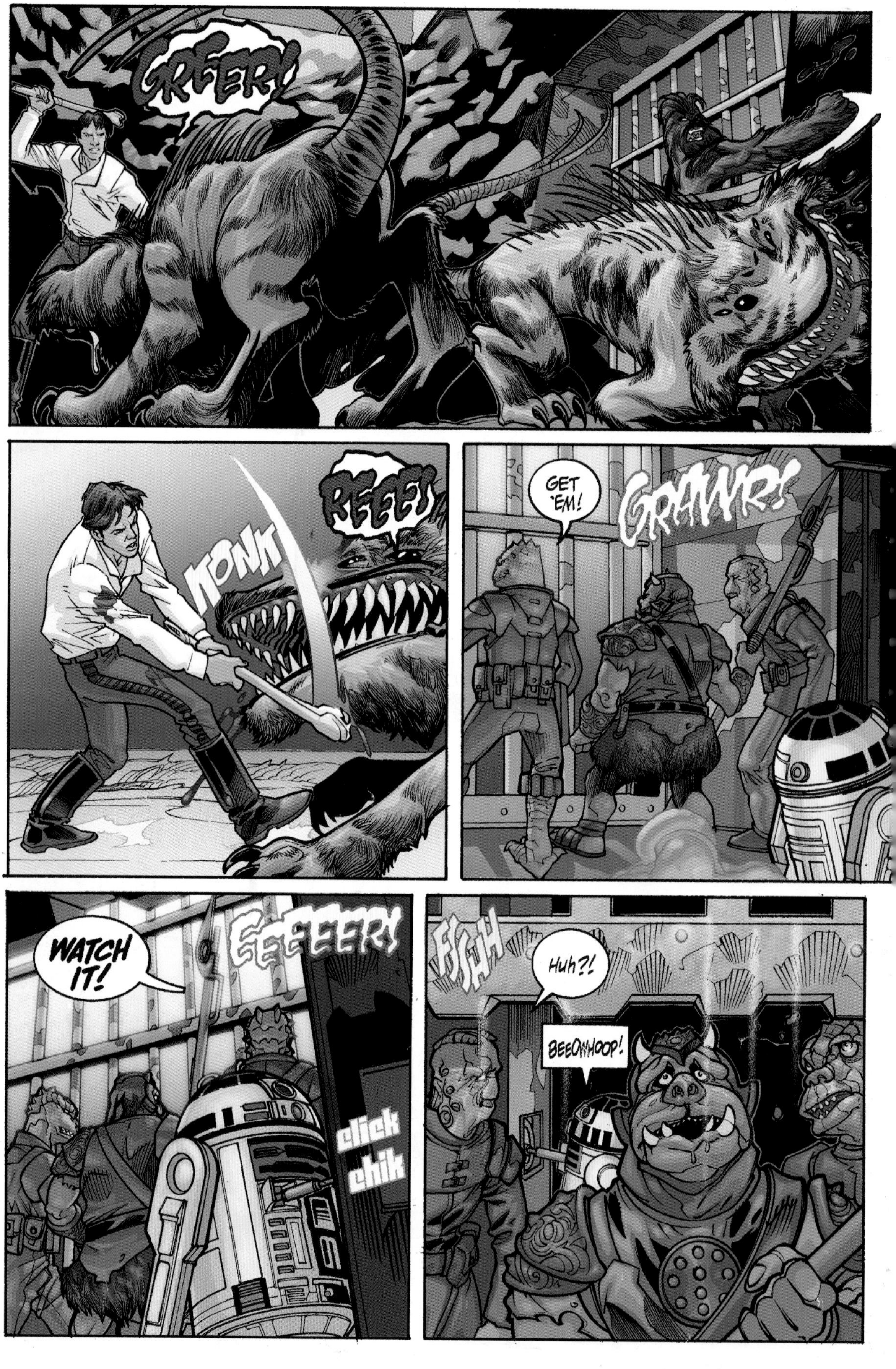
GRFER!
KONK
REEE!
GET 'EM!
GRAWR!
WATCH IT!
EEEEER!
click
chik
FSSH
Huh?!
BEEOWHOOP!

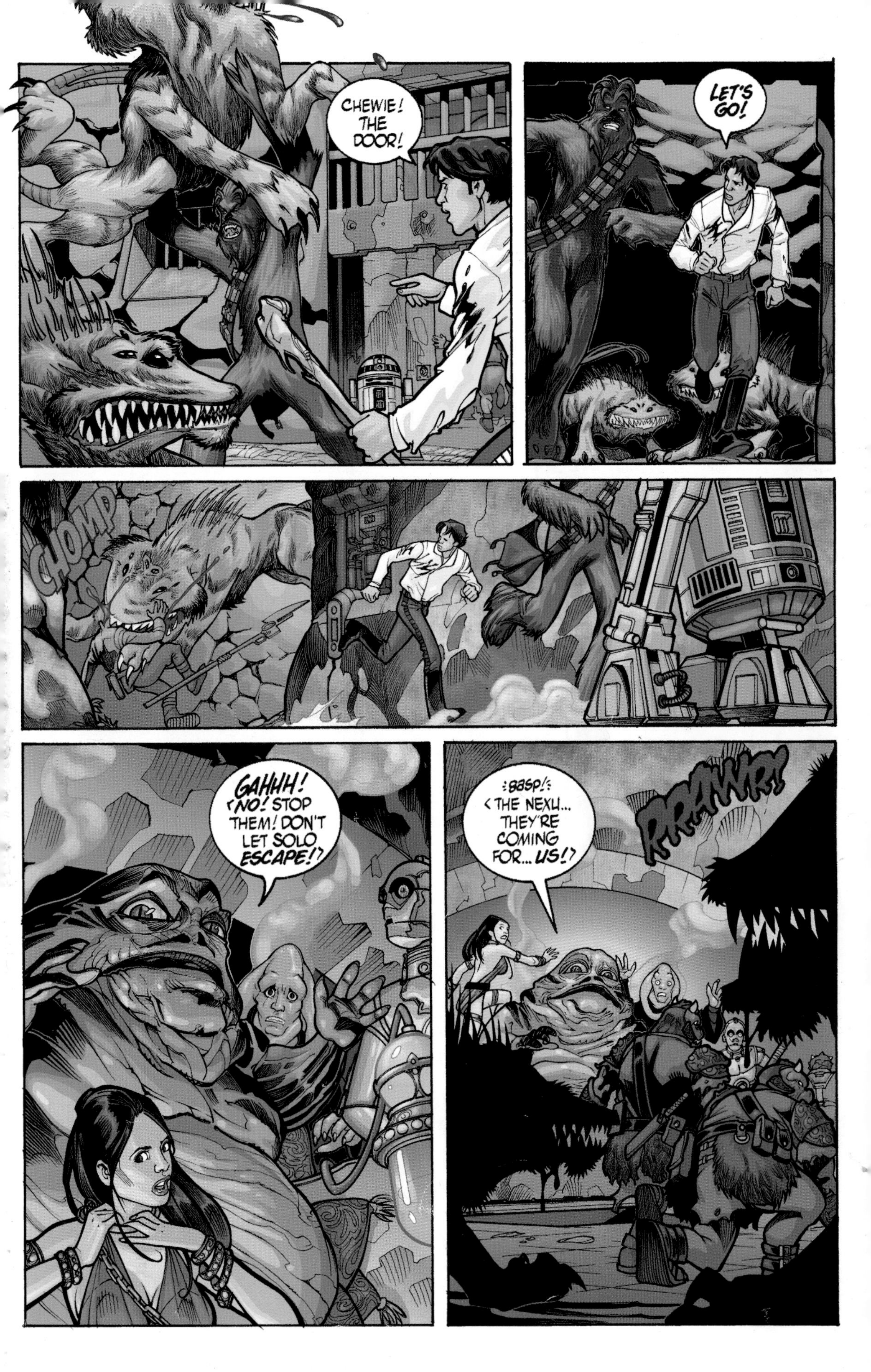

CHEWIE! THE DOOR!
LET'S GO!
CHOMP
GAHHH! ‹NO! STOP THEM! DON'T LET SOLO ESCAPE!›
‹gasp!› ‹THE NEXU... THEY'RE COMING FOR... US!›
RRAWR!

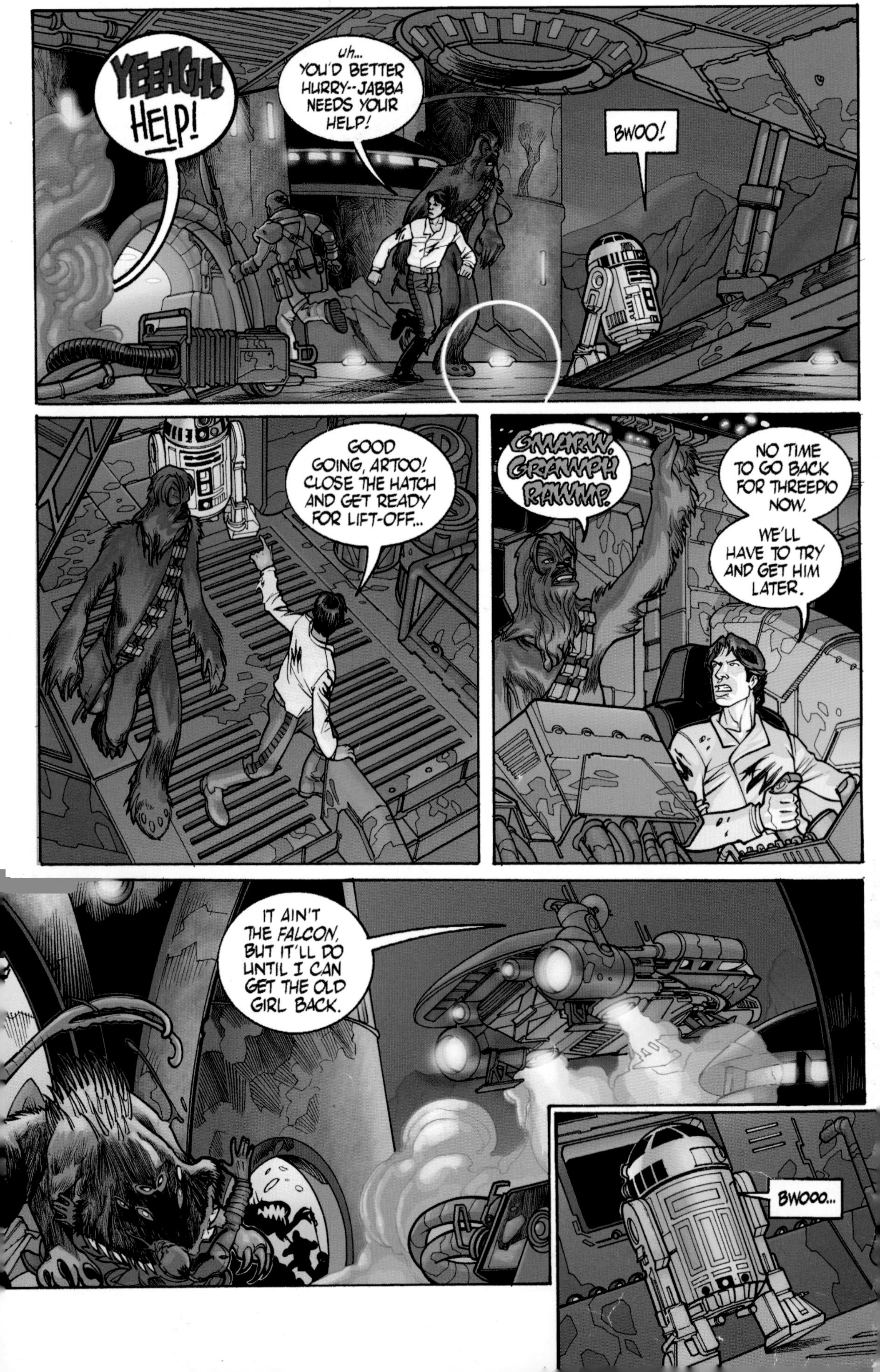
YEEAGH! HELP!
uh... YOU'D BETTER HURRY--JABBA NEEDS YOUR HELP!
BWOO!
GOOD GOING, ARTOO! CLOSE THE HATCH AND GET READY FOR LIFT-OFF...
GWARW. GRAWPH RAWWP.
NO TIME TO GO BACK FOR THREEPIO NOW.
WE'LL HAVE TO TRY AND GET HIM LATER.
IT AIN'T THE FALCON, BUT IT'LL DO UNTIL I CAN GET THE OLD GIRL BACK.
BWOOO...

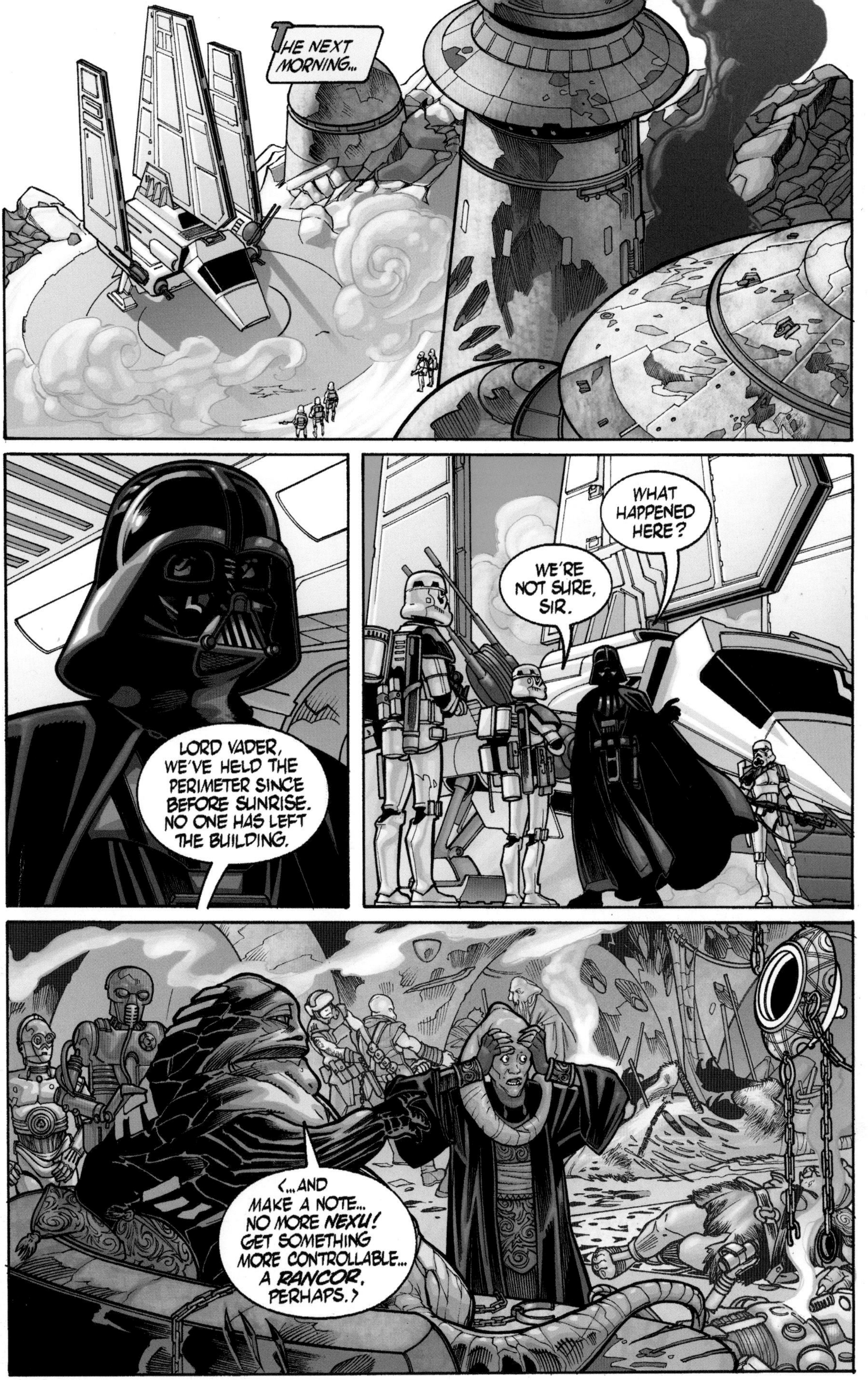
THE NEXT MORNING...
LORD VADER, WE'VE HELD THE PERIMETER SINCE BEFORE SUNRISE. NO ONE HAS LEFT THE BUILDING.
WHAT HAPPENED HERE?
WE'RE NOT SURE, SIR.
<...AND MAKE A NOTE... NO MORE NEXU! GET SOMETHING MORE CONTROLLABLE... A RANCOR, PERHAPS.>

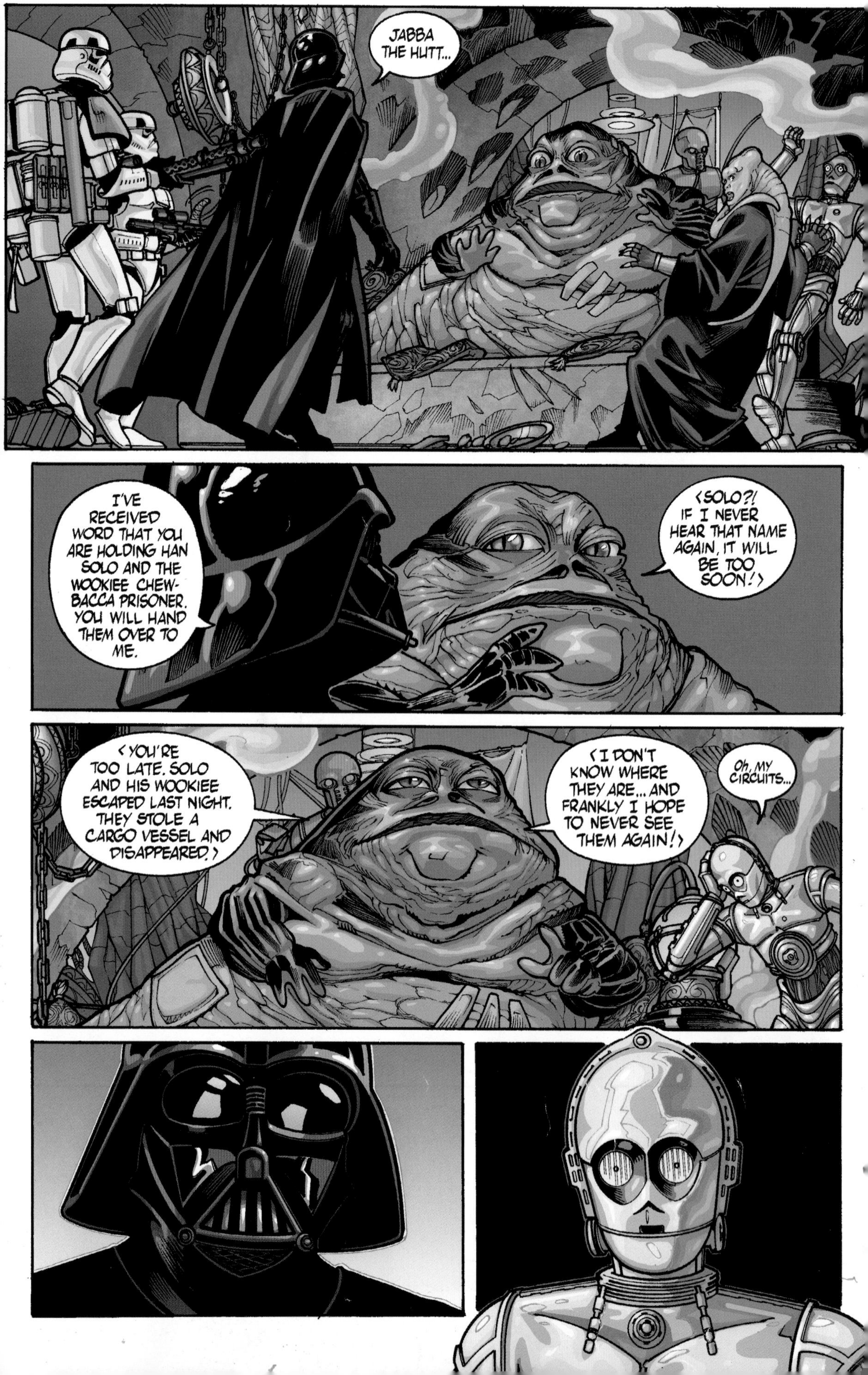
JABBA THE HUTT...
I'VE RECEIVED WORD THAT YOU ARE HOLDING HAN SOLO AND THE WOOKIEE CHEW-BACCA PRISONER. YOU WILL HAND THEM OVER TO ME.
<SOLO?! IF I NEVER HEAR THAT NAME AGAIN, IT WILL BE TOO SOON!>
<YOU'RE TOO LATE. SOLO AND HIS WOOKIEE ESCAPED LAST NIGHT. THEY STOLE A CARGO VESSEL AND DISAPPEARED.>
<I DON'T KNOW WHERE THEY ARE... AND FRANKLY I HOPE TO NEVER SEE THEM AGAIN!>
Oh, MY CIRCUITS...

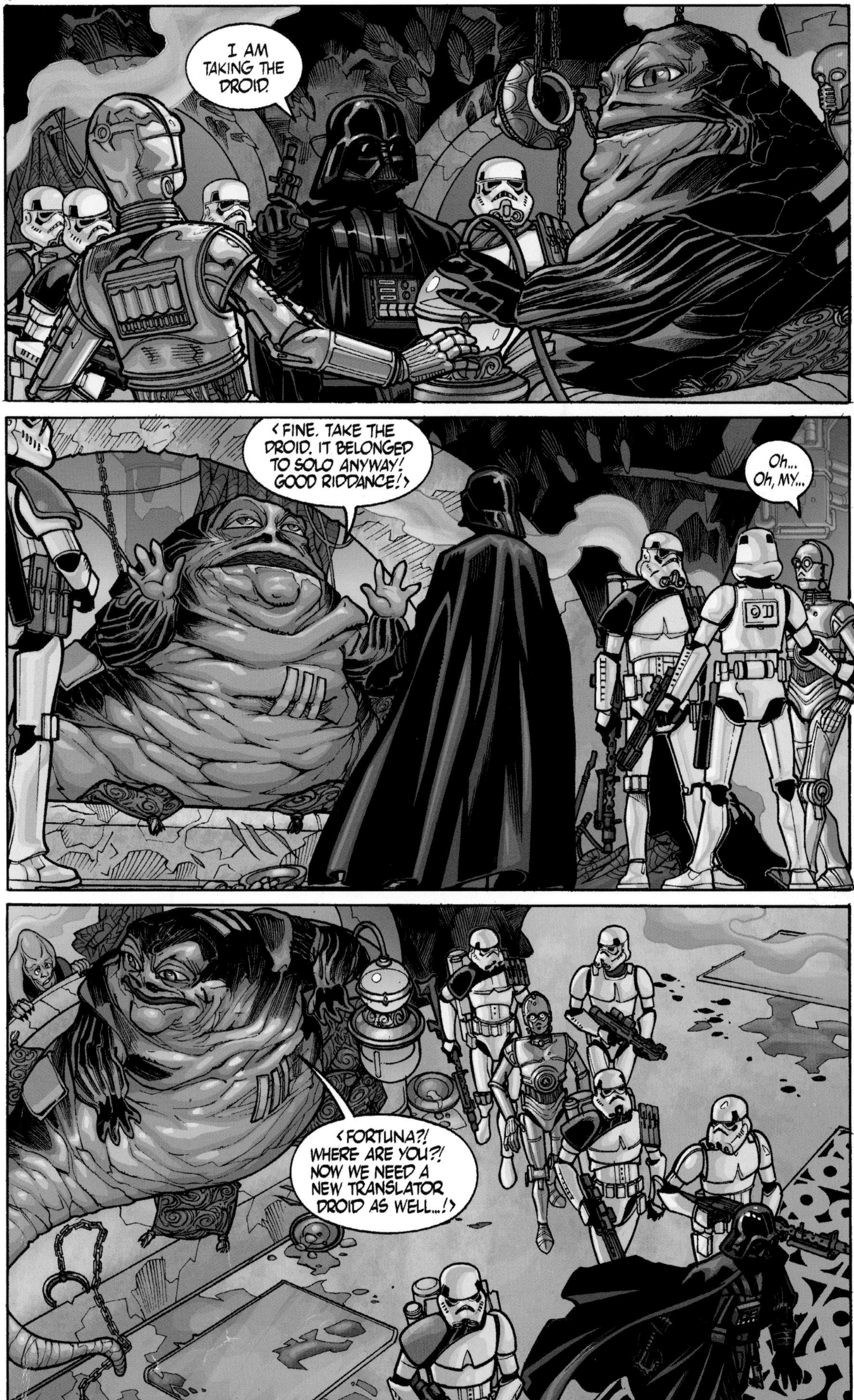
I AM TAKING THE DROID.
‹FINE. TAKE THE DROID. IT BELONGED TO SOLO ANYWAY! GOOD RIDDANCE!›
Oh... Oh, MY...
‹FORTUNA?! WHERE ARE YOU?! NOW WE NEED A NEW TRANSLATOR DROID AS WELL...!›

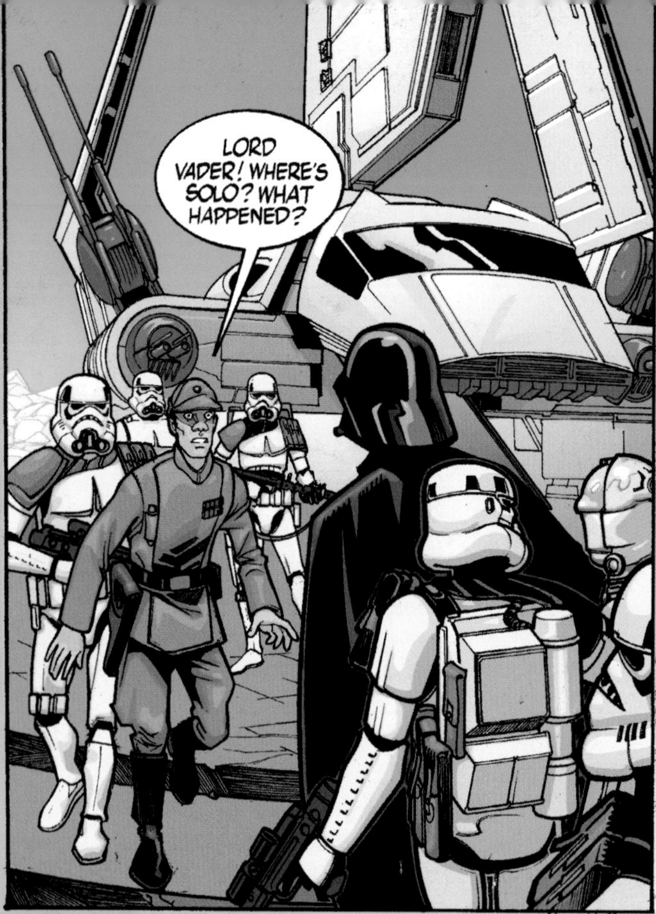
LORD VADER! WHERE'S SOLO? WHAT HAPPENED?

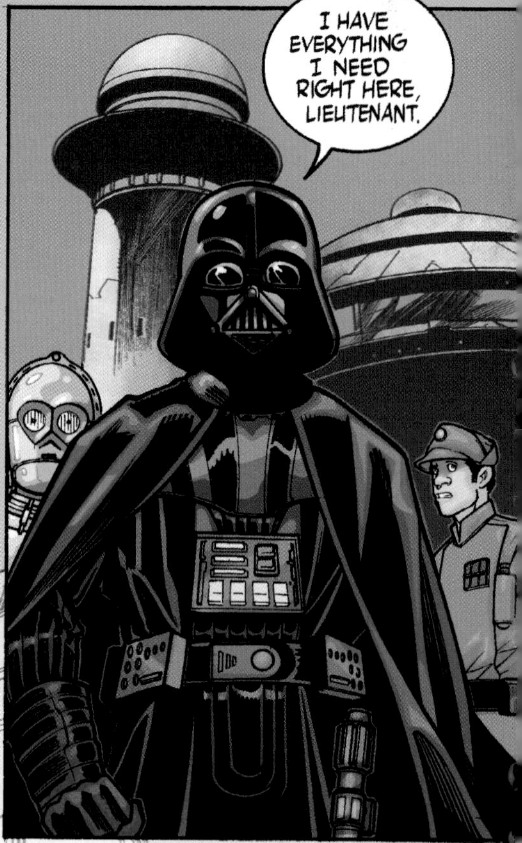
I HAVE EVERYTHING I NEED RIGHT HERE, LIEUTENANT.

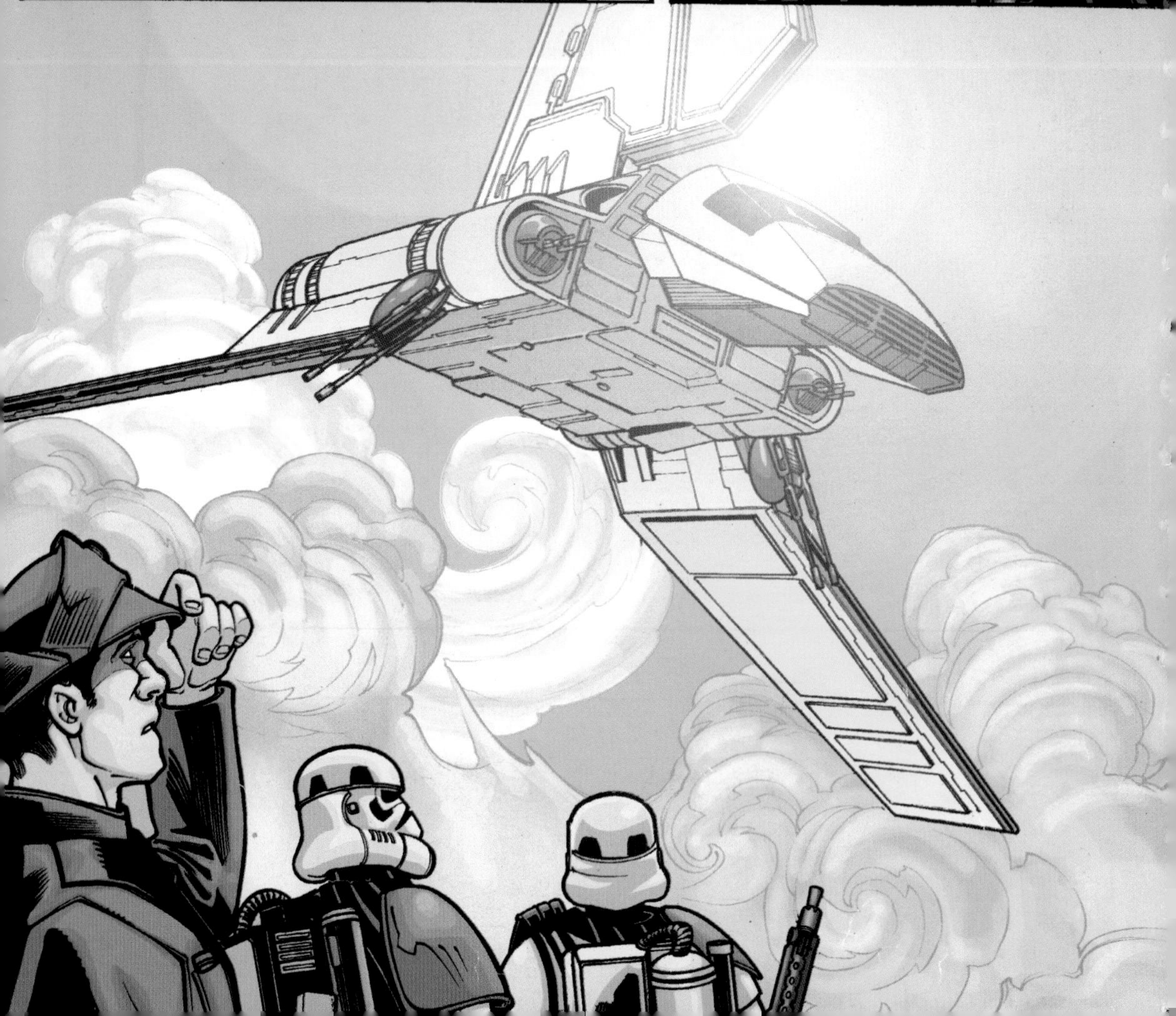

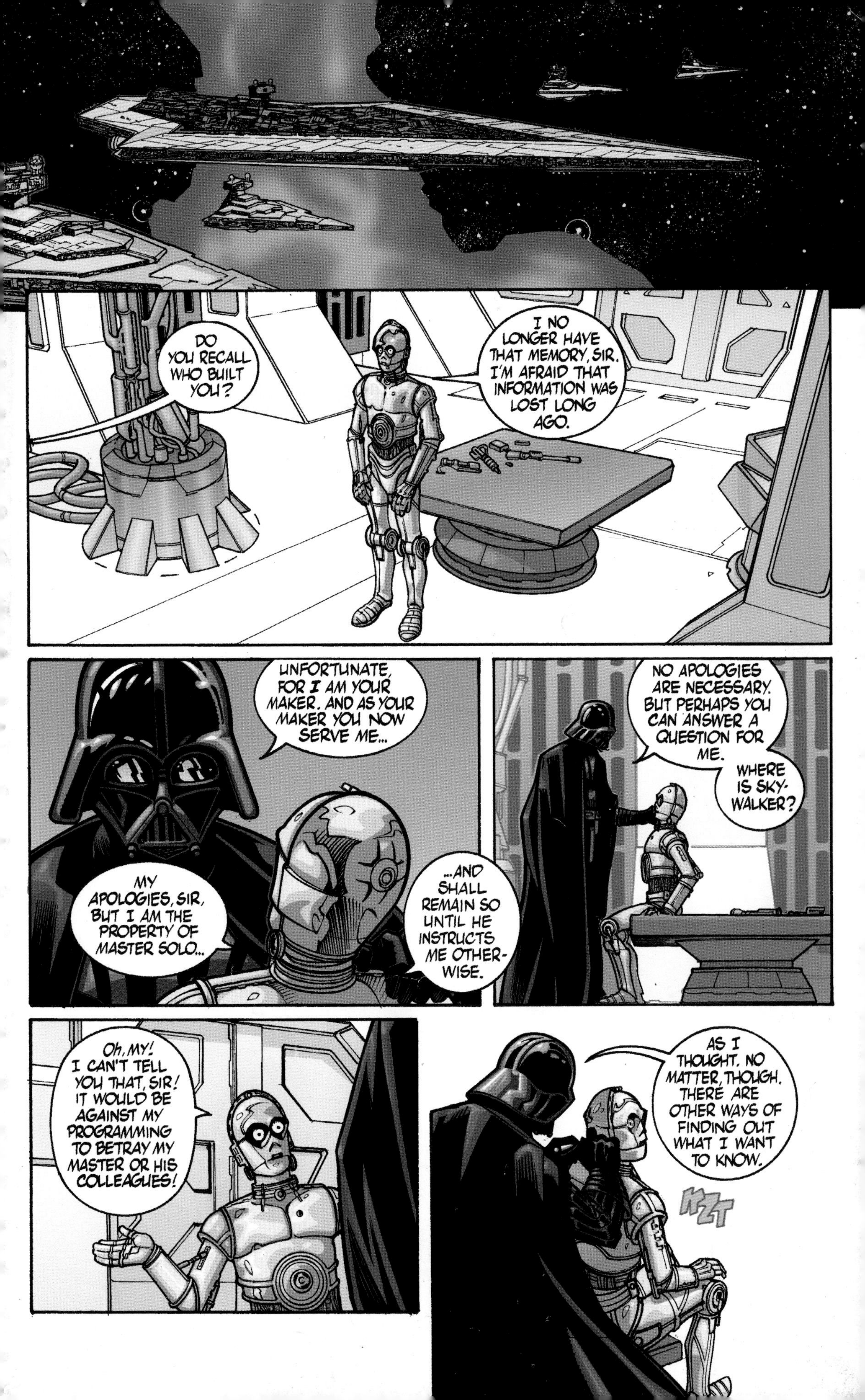
DO YOU RECALL WHO BUILT YOU?
I NO LONGER HAVE THAT MEMORY, SIR. I'M AFRAID THAT INFORMATION WAS LOST LONG AGO.
UNFORTUNATE, FOR I AM YOUR MAKER. AND AS YOUR MAKER YOU NOW SERVE ME...
MY APOLOGIES, SIR, BUT I AM THE PROPERTY OF MASTER SOLO...
...AND SHALL REMAIN SO UNTIL HE INSTRUCTS ME OTHER-WISE.
NO APOLOGIES ARE NECESSARY. BUT PERHAPS YOU CAN ANSWER A QUESTION FOR ME.
WHERE IS SKY-WALKER?
Oh, MY! I CAN'T TELL YOU THAT, SIR! IT WOULD BE AGAINST MY PROGRAMMING TO BETRAY MY MASTER OR HIS COLLEAGUES!
AS I THOUGHT. NO MATTER, THOUGH. THERE ARE OTHER WAYS OF FINDING OUT WHAT I WANT TO KNOW.
KZZT

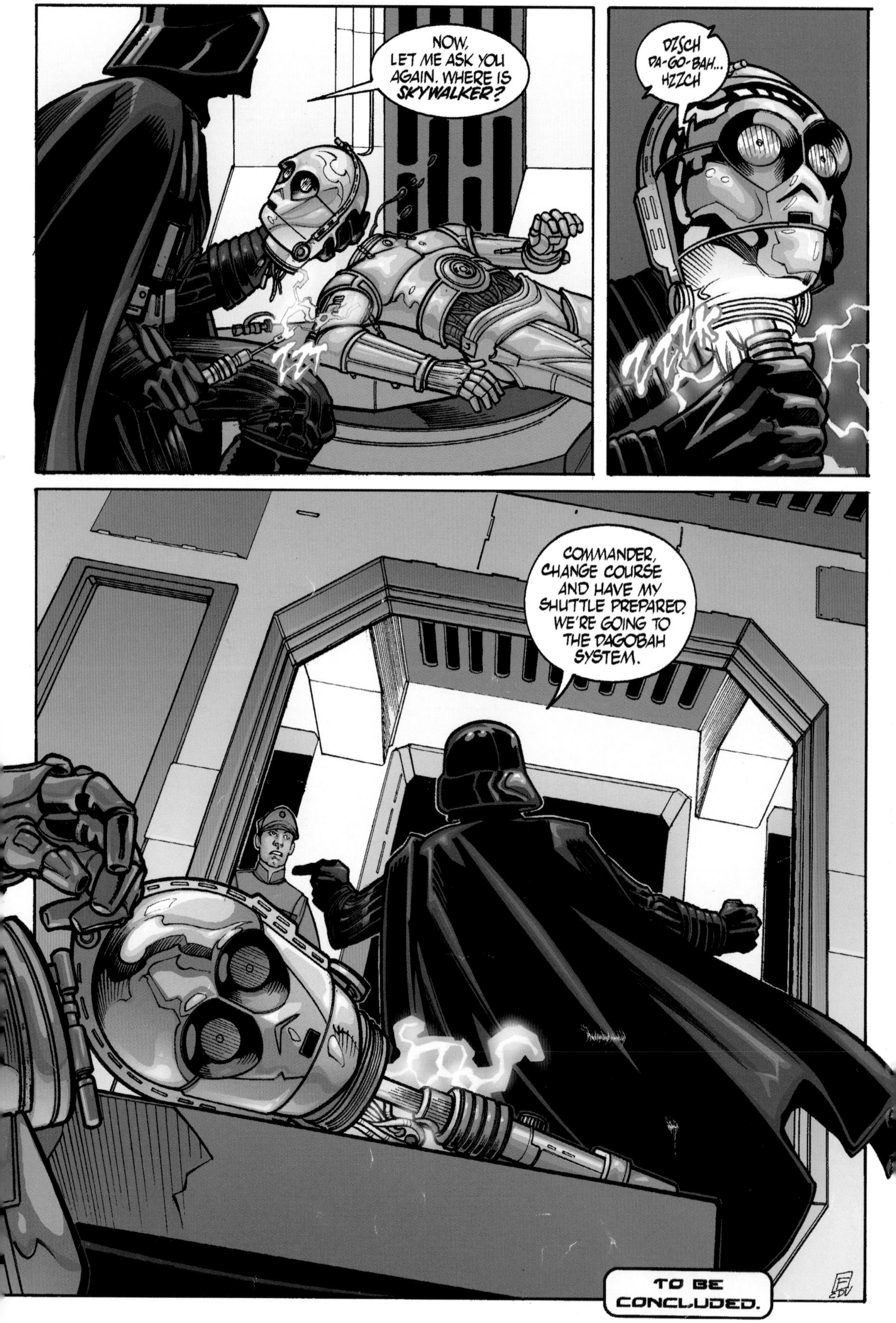
NOW, LET ME ASK YOU AGAIN. WHERE IS SKYWALKER?
ZZT
DZSCH DA-GO-BAH... HZZCH
ZZZZK
COMMANDER, CHANGE COURSE AND HAVE MY SHUTTLE PREPARED. WE'RE GOING TO THE DAGOBAH SYSTEM.
TO BE CONCLUDED.